4/05

Harry's Hats

Written by Ann Tompert • Illustrated by Marcelo Elizalde

Children's Press®
A Division of Scholastic Inc.
New York • Toronto • London • Auckland • Sydney
Mexico City • New Delhi • Hong Kong
Danbury, Connecticut

For J I and J II because...
—A.T.

For Gabriela Keselman
—M.E.

Reading Consultants

Linda Cornwell
Literacy Specialist

Katharine A. Kane
Education Consultant
(Retired, San Diego County Office of Education
and San Diego State University)

Library of Congress Cataloging-in-Publication Data

Tompert, Ann.
  Harry's hats / written by Ann Tompert ; illustrated by Marcelo Elizalde.
      p. cm. — (A Rookie reader)
Summary: A young boy has fun doing different activities depending on
the hat he is wearing each day of the week.
    ISBN 0-516-23613-X (lib. bdg.)   0-516-24647-X (pbk.)
  [1. Hats—Fiction. 2. Days—Fiction.] I. Elizalde, Marcelo, 1953- ill.
II. Title. III. Series.
PZ7.T598Har 2004
[E]–dc22

                                                            2003018659

On Monday, Harry
wore his cowboy hat.

He had fun riding
a horse in the mall.

On Tuesday, Harry wore
his firefighter's hat.

8

He had fun watering the grass, flowers, and trees.

On Wednesday, Harry
wore his baker's hat.

11

He had fun making a cake.

On Thursday, Harry
wore his farmer's hat.

He had fun pulling weeds
and planting seeds.

On Friday, Harry
wore his tall hat.

19

He had fun playing circus
with his dog and cat.

On Saturday, Harry
wore his artist's hat.

He had fun painting
a funny clown.

On Sunday, Harry
wore his baseball hat.

He played ball with his father and mother, and sister and brother.

That was the most fun of all.

Word List (58 words)

a	father	mall	Sunday
all	firefighter's	Monday	tall
and	flowers	most	that
artist's	Friday	mother	the
baker's	fun	of	Thursday
ball	funny	on	trees
baseball	grass	painting	Tuesday
brother	had	planting	was
cake	Harry	played	watering
cat	hat	playing	Wednesday
circus	he	pulling	weeds
clown	his	riding	with
cowboy	horse	Saturday	wore
dog	in	seeds	
farmer's	making	sister	

About the Author

Ann Tompert is an award-winning author of many books. Her love of hats, of which she has almost three dozen, inspired Harry's Hats. Like all of her stories, it was first written in long-hand and then transcribed on her word processor. She lives in a computer-free world in Port Huron, Michigan.

About the Illustrator

To find a hat big enough for Marcelo Elizalde's head has always been hard. Fortunately, he can draw hats to fit any size he needs.